It's My Mission to Make a Definition!

Kelly Doudna

Consulting Editors, Diane Craig, M.A./Reading Specialist
and Susan Kosel, M.A. Education

Published by ABDO Publishing Company, 4940 Viking Drive, Edina, Minnesota 55435.

Printed in the United States.

Credits
Edited by: Pam Price
Curriculum Coordinator: Nancy Tuminelly
Cover and Interior Design and Production: Mighty Media
Photo Credits: AbleStock, BananaStock Ltd., Comstock, Photodisc, ShutterStock, Stockbyte, Wewerka Photography

Library of Congress Cataloging-in-Publication Data

Doudna, Kelly, 1963-
    It's my mission to make a definition! / Kelly Doudna.
      p. cm. -- (Science made simple)
    ISBN 10 1-59928-600-9 (hardcover)
    ISBN 10 1-59928-601-7 (paperback)

    ISBN 13 978-1-59928-600-6 (hardcover)
    ISBN 13 978-1-59928-601-3 (paperback)
    1. Vocabulary--Juvenile literature. 2. Science--Juvenile literature. I. Title. II. Series: Science made simple (ABDO Publishing Company)

PE1449.D67326 2006
428.1--dc22   2006012566

SandCastle Level: Fluent

SandCastle™ books are created by a professional team of educators, reading specialists, and content developers around five essential components—phonemic awareness, phonics, vocabulary, text comprehension, and fluency—to assist young readers as they develop reading skills and strategies and increase their general knowledge. All books are written, reviewed, and leveled for guided reading, early reading intervention, and Accelerated Reader® programs for use in shared, guided, and independent reading and writing activities to support a balanced approach to literacy instruction. The SandCastle™ series has four levels that correspond to early literacy development. The levels help teachers and parents select appropriate books for young readers.

Emerging Readers
(no flags)

Beginning Readers
(1 flag)

Transitional Readers
(2 flags)

Fluent Readers
(3 flags)

These levels are meant only as a guide. All levels are subject to change.

A **definition** helps other people understand what you are talking about. You make a definition when you tell what you know about something.

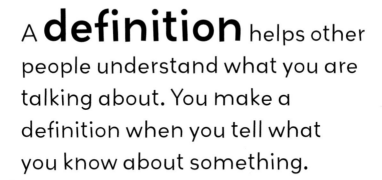

Words used to talk about making a definition:

describe
explain
explanation
information
tell how

3

A is something that has a handle and that you drink from.

A is orange

and is the root of a plant.

 is the solid form of water.

A has scales and fins and swims in the water.

A  has an engine and four wheels.

 shade your

eyes from the sun.

It's My Mission to Make a Definition!

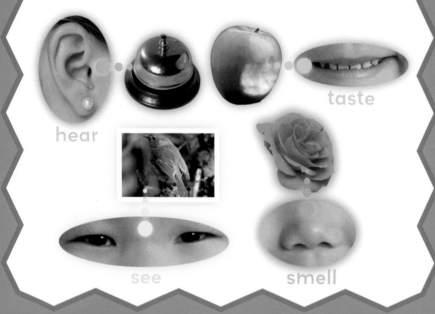

hear

taste

see

smell

Making a definition creates an explanation. Just tell what your senses show. From there your definition will grow.

You don't have to be a magician to come up with a definition.

11

You should feel free
to describe what you see.
Tell how it sounds
or if it walks on the
ground.

I'm thinking
of something with
feathers and wings.
It has two legs
and a beak,
and it sings.

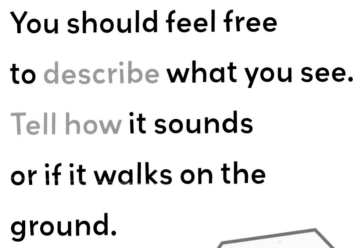

13

14

Others will confirm that they understand the term.
All the information adds up to a definition.

Based on what you heard, did you know that I meant a bird?

We Make Definitions Every Day!

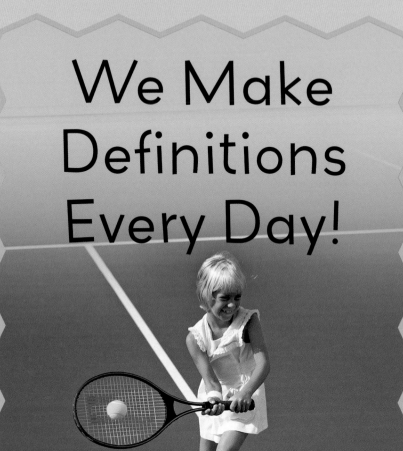

Ellen plays tennis. Tennis is a game. You use a racket to hit a small ball over a net when you play tennis.

Ellen makes a definition when she explains how something is done.

18

Fay rides her bicycle.
A bicycle has a seat
to sit on. It has two
wheels and pedals
to make it go.

Fay makes a
definition when
she describes
what something
looks like.

Carl eats a banana.
A banana is long and
soft. It tastes sweet.

Carl makes a definition when he tells how the banana looks and tastes.

Luis likes music.

He plays the guitar.

What definition could Luis make to describe the guitar?

23

Glossary

confirm – to verify that something is a certain way.

mission – a special job or assignment.

racket – a paddle-shaped frame with a handle and crisscrossing strings that is used to hit a small ball. Also spelled racquet.

term – a word or expression used to describe something.